Seagift 2022

Seagift 2022

Edited by Melinda Tognini, T. C. Shelley and
Miriam Wei Wei Lo

Sheridan Institute of Higher Education

Publisher:
Sheridan Institute of Higher Education
P.O. Box D178
Perth
WA 6849
Australia

Email: seagift@sheridan.edu.au

ISBN: 9780645563603

Seagift was curated and edited on the lands of the Whadjuk people of the Noongar nation. We acknowledge their traditional custodianship and pay our respects to their Elders.

"Many waters cannot quench love, neither can floods drown it."

CONTENTS

INTRODUCTION..1

JACKSON BLACK
Six Minutes Home 3

T. C. SHELLEY
The Road to Bethlehem..7

LAKSHMI R. KANCHI
The Joy of Shattering Glass...10

ELIZABETH LEWIS
Longyi..12

JILLIAN BRETTO
A House of Blue Lanterns..14

MIRIAM WEI WEI LO
Definitions...23

SAMUEL MITCHELL
Excerpt From the Song of Solomon...............................25

JAKE DENNIS
Ima..27

CONTENTS

MELINDA TOGNINI
Winter Solstice...29

NATALIE LEITÃO
My Tent...32

ELLA KURZ
A Mother's Fairytale..34

ANDREW LANSDOWN
A Game of Anything..36

ALCHENNY AGYPUTRI
Essence..37

HOR SHIDE GYATSO (Trans. MIKE RANDALL)
Scripture Reading...45

ALEXANDRA JUSTINICO
To Logan, A Child with San Filippo Syndrome..............47

ANDREW LANSDOWN
The Homecoming...50

MAYA KRAYNEVA
Train to Newcastle..51

NAMLOYAK DHUNGSER
Song of the Seasons...57

ALISON DENCH
Milkfish and Ocean..58

STEPHANIE FELIX
Ants..60

BEN LEE
What Spears Are Good For.................................62

CONTRIBUTORS..68

ACKNOWLEDGEMENTS.............................74

Introduction

Seagift is ... a beginning. It is an inaugural collection of poems, non-fiction, and fiction curated by members of the Creative Writing team at Sheridan Institute of Higher Education.

There is joy in beginning. We are delighted by the way in which writers responded to the theme of joy, which was an optional theme, yet somehow present in every submission. So many of these pieces express the joy of human connection, even if that connection is momentary, troubled, or framed by anxious sorrow. There is joy in doing: in reading, making art, learning a language, observing the seasons, defeating an enemy, making a game out of anything. There is joy in being: with a loved one; or immersed in the landscape, whether outback or suburban. There is *schadenfreude* in the momentary joy of revenge. There is even fake joy in the form of a pill.

Seagift was chosen as a name to evoke the ocean and its gifts: kelp, violet snails, and cuttlebone—tossed onto the shore; so apparently random, like life and art—a disorderly order. We hope to echo one of the ancient creation stories, held by both Jewish and Christian traditions, that depicts God as Spirit hovering over the face of the deep, preparing to do the work of calling this universe into being. *Seagift* also acknowledges the Indian Ocean location of Sheridan Institute in Boorloo/Perth: with all its complex, sometimes-violent-sometimes-graceful, history of interactions between First Nations and Migrant peoples.

Most of the work here is new, but we are also pleased to include two previously published poems by our esteemed colleague Andrew Lansdown.

We thank the people who have made *Seagift* possible: our family and friends, the staff and students of Sheridan Institute, the Creative Writing Hub community, and the wonderful writers whose work is present in this collection. We hope to follow this print edition with an audio version.

Joy is both a practice and an outcome. We hope it may be both for you as you read *Seagift*.

—Miriam Wei Wei Lo, T. C. Shelley, and Melinda Tognini

PS. If you love what we do, please support us by doing any or all the following...

- emailing us at <seagift@sheridan.edu.au> so we can let you know about upcoming *Seagift* projects
- buying this anthology
- buying the audio version when it comes out
- raving about us to all your family and friends, in person, and wherever you hang out digitally!

Six Minutes Home

JACKSON BLACK

The car rumbles to life; Char drops the handbrake, slams it into reverse, and we back out into the street with a roar. The radio clicks to life, starting with Guns N' Roses' album *Appetite for Destruction*. "Paradise City" plays softly. There's no way, with how tired he is, that I'm going to let him drive home early from our annual Delaney-Black family Australia Day dinner on his own.

Once upon a time we spent a lot of time together, before my time was occupied by endless hours of textbooks. Before he worked or had his own social life, we'd sit together while the rest of the family was out, and I would paint, and he would unleash a wall of obnoxious noise. My little brother is a good guitarist: much to my disgust he educated me in the worlds of 70s, 80s, and 90s Rock, Hard Rock and Metal, and in 90s and 2000s Grunge and Alternate Rock. I'd protest again and again about the content of the lyrics and yet he'd continue to ask me what to play next. I always wound up giving him a name – if only so I could get back to my painting.

"Your music's a nice volume for once," I joke.

Charlie, about to turn off of the street, stops and glances at me. The corners of his lips lift slightly. He rarely offers the world a broad grin in the way most people do, instead, a shadow of a smile plays across his lips and around his mouth while his eyes twinkle. When he smiles like that, irony, sarcasm and humour stand ready to be unleashed on all present. He leans over to reach for the radio.

"Right," he drawls, as his fingers spin across the dials, amping the volume up to full noise, the electric guitars and screaming vocals blocking out the roar of the car as we catapult out onto the streets of Armadale, heading home.

The streets are largely empty, the great ghost-gums looming over Armadale Road shadowed and lit by the yellowed glow of streetlights. The music drowns out the rest of the world and as we rocket along the roads I slide along the bench seat, trying to hold myself in place by the cold rough plastic of the handle above. Charlie is a capable, though enthusiastic, driver. His car bounces and lurches like an amusement park ride. He's bobbing his head slightly to the music, his aviators dangling from the neck of his slim-fit shirt. His going-out Akubra skates precariously along the seat between us, and I desperately try not to crush it. His work Akubra hangs from the rack above. He's wearing his chunky, yellow-leather work boots instead of more appropriate going-out footwear. Burn and welding scars peek out from under his shirtsleeves, contrasting against the sun-burnt skin. In this instant he sort of looks like Dad. Yet at the same time, listening to the roaring music, comfortably slouched in the driver's seat, manipulating the gear-stick with a lazy ease, wearing and surrounded by the paraphernalia of his life, he is uniquely himself. Because of it he reminds me of the past.

We rarely spend time together anymore. He's grown. Four weeks into his farriery apprenticeship, months since the last time he and I hung out together, and he is not the same person. He's less talkative and far more exhausted. Tomorrow I'll go back to uni for the year. He'll start another week of work and busy socialising. On the rare occasions we'll spend time together over the coming months it will be in silence, too distracted and tired to spark a conversation. Maybe this is what it means to grow up, to move on? We have our own lives; his of people, events, and working with white-hot metal; mine of games nights, dressage arenas, and endless seas of words and ideas. We've never shared much in common; he was always the bold people person, the centre of every conversation, while I was always the spectral older brother, looming at the edge. Once, I could rely on him to draw the attention and focus away from me. We could bicker, argue, and be brothers. We could have each other's backs. Yet now we walk our separate paths. So I treasure the little moments and silent, short car trips where we spend time together without needing to say anything.

At the Southwest Hwy intersection, the half-shadowed glare of an older lady in the car beside us breaks me out of my reminiscing. She mustn't like the loud music and I can't handle the introspection any-more. I pause for a moment and glance over at Char, who's staring at the lights, clearly wishing they'd turn green. I let the fatigue and racing thoughts sink in for a moment. With the start of the year's classes to-morrow, I can't handle this right now. I need to be focussed and driven, energetic. Certainly not bogged down with musings and nostalgia. It'd be better if I handled this later. At some point. Maybe. And so instead of dealing with the past and facing the future, something snaps inside of me and I let the escapism take over. I can't hide in it forever but I might as well try, till I don't need to be in control. Until I'm on top of study. Until I'm not tired. Until I'm not frustrated.

Time to live in the moment.

Out of nowhere I start to howl out the familiar chorus of the song. Charlie doesn't even glance my way; he just winces with every bellowed, off-key syllable and slides his foot onto the accelerator as the lights flick to green.

I sing raucously as the song begins to wind up, and our trip nears its conclusion. I gesture to a side-road.

"Take the long route home," I yell at Char. He smiles again and swerves up the night-black street, hitting the accelerator to steam up the hill, racing down into the creek-gully, then flooring the pedal again in order to race up to the top of our street: it's an exceptionally short excuse for a detour, but a longstanding favourite of ours. Then we roll back down the slope and around the bend to slide gracefully into our drive. I lean over to him and rest a hand on his shoulder.

"Love you mate," I mumble before he, as usual, deftly shrugs me away. I swing open the door, loosening each slightly-clenched muscle as I clamber from his car, then drag open the gate while "Paradise City" comes to an end. The night is dead black above and around us as the dull roar of the engine shuts off and I close the gate. I need to sleep before the rollercoaster of study begins tomorrow.

The Road to Bethlehem

T. C. SHELLEY

My Father, I sit here
     on the side of the road staring at my hands,
While she, sweet smiling girl, wanders the long grass
     to do what pregnant women do.
It is too too long a journey on a hard-backed donkey,
     we do not take many rests.
She doesn't complain, just shakes her head and we go on.

Sometimes she says she'd rather walk,
     although the skin under her eyes is a weary brown
        and she plods with the same slow tread
          as the donkey.

She turns and kisses its nose and pets its ears
     as if it is the best creature in this dry land,
And I wonder if she sees me with the same kind eyes.
I am simply a mule of a man,
     a small one, a beast of the field,
        one meant to carry her on to another place.

Father, she has the sweetest smile.

I'm here, Lord, wondering what is waiting for me
    in Bethlehem, I study my hands
        as if they might teach me.
They are rough hands, calloused,
    with wrists as brown and hard as oiled wood.
        A carpenter's hands.

I do not think they are the right hands
    for the father of a god-king.
Or the husband of a maiden mother.
It should be a man with soft hands and a hard heart,
    to teach the boy the strategies of rulers and monarchs,
Smooth hands to write edicts and lessons;
    to calculate the numbers of war and warriors.
I sometimes think I am here to deliver them both
    into the hands of a better man.
        Someone powerful.
        Respected.
        Confident.
I have not played the husband, she owes me nothing,
And maybe that's your will, Lord.

Yet I remember her small face, her gentle, smiling face, and I hope.

Others pass on the way to census,
    in pairs and trios, family groups and caravans,
Each is one less room available to us,
She should have clean linen and a midwife to cool her brow,
    offer her comforts and consolation.
You have a room prepared for her, don't you, Lord?
I worry she may give birth out here in the dirt and muck,

And she seems so sure of me.
At night, she sleeps with her head on my arm,
     her steady breath falling in and out as I stare at the sky,

I see a growing star winking at me, but I cannot sleep
     and I too tread with donkey weary steps.

While on the road, I see the work Romans give to carpenters,
Two hard pieces of wood, pressed together, to kill a man slowly.
On some stretches of road, they grow like trees.
You would not want your son to waste his life on these.
So how can a carpenter father the son of God?

The grass rustles and she returns.
My smiling girl.

I look at my hands.
I look at my hands.

The Joy of Shattering Glass

LAKSHMI R. KANCHI

It is a fact that when glass breaks
the cracks travel at speeds
of over 3,000 miles per hour.

Of course, I don't think of this
when pain and anger are still dangerously,
deliciously coursing through my veins.

When your favourite glass,
an exquisite old-fashioned tumbler from Italy,
hits the floor and your smile ceases.

When whiskey spills, splintered shards
break free, travel fast and deep.
Rage wins. Love loses.

In that moment,
the joy of shattering glass
is bigger than the both of us.

Even when we make up, that empty spot
on the shelf where your glass was once kept,
grins and teases – vacant yet adamant.

Quietly, tempting us to   indulge.

Longyi

ELIZABETH LEWIS

Thirty long years of curry down the hall,
wafting to bedrooms,
fingers gentle and steaming
smooth over the checked wool blanket
on the bed, the child napping there.

Big family, always grandchildren
for sleepovers,
tiptoe to the pot on the stove,
the long
inhale,
spice soaks into skin.

It means wrapping up in a longyi
borrowed from Grandpa for
multicultural day to show where
you come from.

I carry my family inside me, my hands over the cooking
now, so much ginger, turmeric, so much time.
"You can't be in a hurry making curry,"
my Grandma speaks, her words from my lips.

My Grandpa shakes a jar of peanuts in my direction.
His mind has gone on ahead of him, leaving
his body with only a small handful of knowing,
"I know you," he says,
"Yes Grandpa, it's me."
"You're the sweet one."

He wraps around me,
warm and smelling of home.

A House of Blue Lanterns

JILLIAN BRETTO

The blue festival lanterns strung up across the streets should have been bright and dancing in the wind. Se Ria refused to look up at them as she walked down the stone path. If she did, all she would see would be unlit lanterns hanging sadly in the still air. Growing up, the *Goykhir* festival season had been her favourite time of year. The streets would be teeming with people and sounds of laughter and music, while the aroma of festival foods filled the air. Se Ria turned a corner, exited the archway, and halted as something lightly hit her in the face. She blinked and took a quick step back. A string of lanterns had come untied from the edge of the upward curved roof and now lay across the archway, motionless and unlit.

Of all the festival decorations, Se Ria loved the lanterns the most. Mama had told her the story of Al Va Yah, the famed peace bringer who had brought an end to the Vyun-Tal War. Legend has it that after Va Yah had negotiated the treaty and when the blood oath ritual had been finished, a drop of her blood had fallen onto the lantern flame. The light from the white lantern had glowed blue as the flame burned for a moment before spluttering out. When Uncle Fio frowned and said that it wasn't possible, Mama had only laughed. She had pointed out that he was barely older than Se Ria, it was too early for him to start doubting the old folk tales. The stories of Va Yah had been told at every *Goykhir*[1] festival as far as she could remember.

Se Ria sighed and ran her fingers lightly over the lantern before ducking under the string. The end of the string lay dejectedly on the ground. She reached down to pick it up and stopped. What did it matter if the decorations had come undone? She might as well leave it as it was. *All the ornaments would have to be taken down anyway.* She shifted the textbooks tucked in the crook of her arm and wiped a small bead of sweat from her neck. As a country, Vyun wasn't normally warm, not like the north of Tal or humid like Jeyorn, but today the air lay heavy over the city, as if the news of the Emperor had halted any semblance of a breeze.

The news had certainly brought all the festival preparations to a standstill. The Empress had looked tearful but poised on the big screen at the university where the message had aired. Se Ria recalled the Empress's face; her big grey eyes had watered, but she had dabbed at them with a lace scarf as though to prevent any tears from falling. The disarrayed hairs that fell around her face, which Se Ria was sure had been artfully arranged, gave the impression she had come straight from the Emperor's bedside to do the transmission. The screen hadn't captured the chill Se Ria got every time she had been in the Empress's presence, but Se Ria still had shivered when she stood in the campus common area watching the broadcast with her classmates.

Se Ria couldn't help but wonder if the Empress was secretly pleased that there wouldn't be any *Goykhir* festival this year. After all the Empress was from Tal, she couldn't be expected to enjoy taking part in a festival that celebrated the defeat of her country. The news that the Emperor's health had gotten worse had dampened the spirits of the people. A month ago, the imperial physicians had seemed hopeful that he would recover enough to preside over the lantern lighting ceremony, but with the news of his decline the ceremony had been cancelled. Se Ria shook away her thought and focused on the path. One last corner and she would be home.

Se Ria slowly turned her rusty key in the keyhole of her front door and nodded at the guard stationed at the end of the street. After raising her hand to salute the Imperial crest above the door frame, she stepped inside. Laying her armful of textbooks on the entryway table, she let her backpack fall to the floor and bent to replace her dust-covered shoes with her indoor slippers. An odd feeling came over her.

I didn't leave them here.

Se Ria cocked her head to one side, frowning.

I'm sure I left my slippers by the door this morning, not on the rug.

A faint noise sounded from the corner of her apartment, where her bedroom was tucked away. In the silence the familiar creak of her rickety old armchair sounded louder than she remembered. It only made that noise when someone was sitting in it. It seemed she wasn't alone.

Se Ria steeled herself against the apprehension fluttering in her throat. She picked up her slippers with one hand. With the other, she reached behind and pulled a long, thin dagger from a hidden compartment at the base of her bag.

Why hadn't the guard alerted me that I had visitors? She thought to herself, creeping into the hall inch by inch. *I'm walking into a possible danger here. Is this a trap?*

A shiver ran down her spine as a thought occurred to her.

Guards can be bought.

Se Ria stiffened. If this turned out to be that persistent reporter who kept hounding her for an interview, she would slit his throat first, and then the guard's.

Treading slowly over the carpet floor, she made her way to the door of her bedroom. Se Ria peered in the room and tried to catch sight of the mirror that hung in the corner, to see what was waiting for her. Instructions echoed in her mind, snippets of things she had learned from the university's self-protection training.

The instructor had been firm and serious. "Don't go into a fight blind," he had said, chuckling to himself, as though the idea of the well-dressed students throwing punches amused him. "But remember," came the rest of his sentence after he had sobered up, "this is for self-defence. Do not put the peace at risk for the sake of a selfish desire to fight."

Se Ria shifted to get a better angle of the view reflected in the mirror. A lump lay on her bed motionless, and a figure sat in the creaky armchair facing towards the bed. Her curtains had been pulled tightly together to block out most of the light. Se Ria clenched her jaw and adjusted the grip on her dagger.

Two of them?

She waited for her eyes to adjust to the darkness and leaned slightly to get a better view. The form on her bed appeared to be a lady, with a hand tucked under her cheek and long golden hair spread out over Se Ria's freshly cleaned pillows. Se Ria gritted her teeth again. She focused on the figure by the bed. A man with dark hair sat gazing down at the sleeping woman with his chin propped in his hand. Se Ria let out a long breath. The woman was too busy sleeping and the man was too busy staring at her for either of them to be thieves. Or reporters, for that matter.

A stray sunbeam snuck past a crack in the curtains and rested on the man's face. All she could see of his features was a small smattering of dots near the corner of his mouth. The light caught on his hand and a flash of gold blinded her momentarily. Se Ria's eyes narrowed as she focused again. The ring had the family crest. It was the one she'd given to her uncle.

She threw the door open and strode inside. Zom[2] Fio El's eyes snapped up to hers.

"How did you get in here?" she demanded.

Her uncle raised a finger to his lips, motioning to the lady on the bed. Se Ria frowned and opened her mouth again. She didn't care who this woman was or why she was in her bed. A few quick strides brought her zom around. He clamped a hand over Se Ria's mouth and dragged her out of the room. After closing the door as gently as he could with the squirming Se Ria in his grip, Zom Fio led her across the hall and into the kitchen.

Se Ria shrugged out of his grip and rounded on him, the dagger still in her hand. "How did you get in here, Zom Fio?"

"Okay, just listen ... " He trailed off and sighed through his teeth, raking a hand through his hair.

Se Ria waved her hand dismissively. "You know what, I don't care." She paced restlessly across the room. "Why are you here? And who is she?" She jabbed the dagger in the direction of the room.

Her uncle stopped messing up his hair and sank into a nearby dining chair. Se Ria lingered on her feet for a moment, still annoyed by the discovery of her uninvited guests, before taking a seat opposite him. A wry smile played around Zom Fio's mouth. He nodded his chin toward the bedroom door. "She's the oldest daughter of the Jeyorn Crown Prince."

Se Ria stared at him for a moment in shock. A beat of silence passed. And another. And another.

He couldn't be serious.

At length she opened her mouth to speak but all that came out was a hiss. "Are you insane?"

"Be quiet. You'll wake her." He looked towards the bedroom again, as if the golden-haired lady would hear them.

"*What were you thinking?*" she repeated under her breath, flattening her hands on the table. "You kidnapped the Crown Princess?"

He jerked back, surprise in his eyes. "Of course not. We ah, um..." He bent his head and finished the rest of his sentence too softly for Se Ria to hear.

"You what? What have you done now?"

He slightly raised his head, but still not meeting her eyes. "We, uh ... we eloped."

She closed her eyes for a moment and took a deep breath. "Now I know you've really lost it." He frowned at her. Zom Fio opened his mouth, but Se Ria pre-empted him. "Why did you bring her here?"

"I didn't have anywhere else to take her. You're the only person that I have left in Vyun that I can trust." As if that made it all better.

"And you thought you'd be safe *here*?" Se Ria threw up her hands in exasperation. "The comments you made about the Empress stirred up the factions and the insurgents. You do realize that, don't you? She's going to be out for your blood."

Zom Fio gritted his teeth. "I thought I told you to be quiet. Let me explain."

Se Ria leaned back in her chair, arms folded, and took him in slowly. The last time she had seen her Uncle Fio, he had been in high spirits, recently returned from his mandatory military service. Less than a year later he had left to serve under the diplomats stationed in Jeyorn. The occasional photos she had seen of him in the newspapers always appeared as if he had all his business in order; he never had so much as a hair out of place. He was always smiling and always impeccably dressed. Nothing like the young man sitting across the table from her now. Dark circles clung around his eyes, and light stubble dusted his chin. His clothes, usually spotless and fitted, hung awkwardly on his frame. Now that she looked closer, he looked ... exhausted.

Zom Fio leaned forward and leant to the table, clasping his hands together. "We got married three months ago in Jeyorn." He gave a tiny smile at the surprise on Se Ria's face.

Se Ria didn't keep up with news or gossip about the royal families overseas, but she did follow her uncle's diplomatic career. How had she not noticed that her uncle had fallen for Princess Yevji? There had not been even a hint about the match in the scandal sheets.

"And you couldn't keep staying over there as you were *because* ... ?"

His brow furrowed as he leaned back in the chair. "A month ago, she started having night visions." Se Ria raised an eyebrow. "Visions about a boy with gold markings, dressed in blue robes."

Oh.

Oh boy.

Fifteen Months Later

As far as escape plans went, this wasn't a particularly good one. There were too many variables, too many things that could go wrong.

But at this point, it was all she had.

Se Ria summoned what she hoped was a casual, curious demeanour as she stepped out onto the small balcony. She had only a few moments to observe the outside before she would be hustled back into the room. As if anyone would bother to climb up five stories to kill her.

"Someone had already 'bothered' to assassinate Zom Fio El," a little voice taunted inside.

She made a show of stretching her arms slightly before leaning on the handrail and looking down. The team of Queensguard that had been assigned to her after her uncle's assassination were probably already in position. Some were at the entrance of the apartments across the road, dressed as gardeners and repairmen, some at the café trying their best to blend in like locals. Se Ria knew there would be others within her own apartment complex, making it difficult to escape.

"Your Highness, please come inside."

Se Ria buried a flicker of annoyance at the order. *Not even a full minute outside. I need more time to see where they are.*

She turned with an innocent smile to see Val Tai, a middle-aged queensguard, regarding her with a slight frown. Se Ria inclined her head slightly before making her way back through the open sliding door, unhurried, taking one last glance over her shoulder.

"Your Highness, we need to go over your schedule for toda—" Val Tai broke off at a cry from the bedroom.

Se Ria quickly hid the relief she felt at hearing Zo Ra cry and seized the chance to hurry away from the guard. Val Tai wasn't fond of children; she had never so much as given the baby a hint of a smile.

Zo Ra raised his chubby fists when he saw Se Ria approach his cot, drool trickling from his toothless grin. She picked him up and lay him on the bed.

"Hello my darling." She cooed at him.

Zo Ra gave her a cheerful gurgle in reply.

Laying a hand on his ribcage to keep his shirt down, she quickly changed his wet napkin. Se Ria never felt at ease with the guards in the apartment. No one had ever come while she was changing Zo Ra, but all it would take was one moment for someone to discover his hidden mark. One glance would be enough for the queensguards to know that Zo Ra's golden mark signalled him as the next Emperor.

After fixing a quick change of clothes for the child, Se Ria returned to the kitchen with him on her hip, turning him to face away from Val Tai.

Se Ria could feel the scorn radiate from the guard whenever she looked at the baby. In the guard's eyes, he was an illegal child, only alive because of the blood that ran through his veins. People simply did not have children whenever they chose, not without written permission from the Bureau of Family Affairs and a few subtle bribes disguised as fees. Those who couldn't afford the fees were scheduled for terminations. Members of the Imperial Family, no matter how minor, were not exempt from the law.

And yet ...

And yet, Zo Ra's existence was proof that even the royals could flout the law if they chose.

Glossary:

1. *Goykhir* – a festival that is celebrated in the latter part of the year. The people of Vyun celebrate the end of the war with Tal and the beginning of the peacetimes.

2. *Zom* – maternal uncle

Definitions

MIRIAM WEI WEI LO

If love is a choice, what is joy?
      (especially when there is anguish)

It isn't a bubble rising in the chest – that's hope.
It isn't the fleeting burst of sunshine
or the surge of endorphins flooding the brain – that's happiness.

But it could be the sun – simply in its burning.

I stride across the morning of the world:
a green field, endlessly stretching.
The dog is a black and white streak:
an arrow of tooth and claw towards the ball
that comes loping back, tail waving like a flag.

      I am coming to the city, but not to see you.
      We manage dinner, once, but you're right,
      we don't see each other.

(dear God, what *is* joy?)

Yes, the dog, simply in its running.
Yes, my legs, striding across the field.

And yes, the sun, still burning, sweetly, fiercely.

Excerpt From the Song of Solomon

SAMUEL MITCHELL

He
stands holding a bamboo whirligig
my cousin bought in Bali.

She
stands, cuttings in hand,
giving orders.

They
are surrounded
by forty-five year old fruit trees,
week-old flowers,
and dripping foliage.

A breeze speaks,
the bamboo answers.
Laughter and silliness
sing their song.

And it is obvious
to anyone who cares to notice—
my Grandparents
are
in
love.

Ima

JAKE DENNIS

For Stephanie

After the shower, they move inside sunlight,
awake as babies behind their new home,
its terracotta roof freshly darkened, cleaned.
He wets his dry *sumi* from still-drinking grass,
loosens its pine soot and clinging albumen proteins,
washing away its newness in her heirloom *suzuri*,
deepening the grind, setting the treasure aside.

Now, she lays blank *washi* on *Community News*,
beneath his *bunchin*, sips whisked matcha, letting yesterday slide
away from her lips, while wind pulls moisture
from bark, as he dips and drags into their dye
a kolonok's coat, then holds the bamboo *fude*
to brush into breath the rising, falling strokes of a roof,
the dash of a joist or head, the angled profile of a figure below.

Then like a child he turns to show her
as unceasing trains of air and the morning sun
lighten the dark wetness while she stands
beside *sakura*. His mind preserves the print
while he waits on her eyes until
the breeze lifts the paper's edges
and a crow like a motor blots the sky.

Japanese:

ima: "now"
sumi: ink stick
suzuri: ink stone
washi: traditional Japanese paper
bunchin: paperweight
fude: brush
sakura: cherry blossom

Winter Solstice

MELINDA TOGNINI

My husband weaves between other vehicles in peak-hour traffic as my groans rise with the crest of my next contraction.

This pregnancy has been fraught with worry since a routine ultrasound revealed not only that we were having a girl but that she would be born with a broken heart. How blue will she be when she is born? How quickly will she need medical intervention? Will doctors be able to save her? Right now, though, I'm wondering whether I'll make it to the hospital in time for the intravenous antibiotics I've been prescribed.

Despite the current waves of pain, I am ready. Not prepared exactly, because how can you be prepared for the road we're about to head down? But ready to step out of the limbo and the unknown of the past five months.

Dusk descends on this mid-winter day as Luke slides the car into a 'Set-down Only' bay outside the hospital. Rain brushes my hair as Luke guides me through the front doors and into the lobby. Someone slips a wheelchair beneath me and manoeuvres me towards the lift and up to the birthing suite.

In the end, there is no time for antibiotics nor the epidural I'd pre-booked. In too much of a rush to wait for the obstetrician's arrival from the other side of town, our daughter is caught by a nurse as I lean over the bed, grunting and pushing.

She's not making any noise. I hold my breath. *Shouldn't she be crying?*

And then she is bellowing.

I exhale.

"Nothing wrong with her lungs," says the paediatrician.

The nurse wraps the baby snugly before placing her on my chest as if this was any normal birth. I stare into my daughter's blue eyes; she seems remarkably unimpressed with the turn of events.

All too quickly, she is rushed off downstairs to the special care nursery, Luke following close behind.

There is a photo taken less than an hour after she's born. She's lying in a clear Perspex cot; someone has found a tiny yellow beanie, which now adorns her head. And Sam, who's just turned four, is gazing with amazement and delight at this tiny being that is his sister.

"Her name is Jayne," he tells the nurse.

Even now, seventeen years later, joy emanates from this photo that sits above my desk. A reminder that at one time, my son was enraptured with his baby sister. Before he realised that this creature would need so much extra care, would unknowingly steal the attention that had been almost entirely his until now.

I am not in this scene. I'm still upstairs in the birthing suite with the obstetrician, who has arrived just in time to stitch up my second-degree tear.

"I can't get here in twenty minutes in peak-hour traffic," she says by way of apology.

**

Later that evening, after Luke has taken Sam home to bed, I am wheeled down to see my daughter. Despite how seriously ill she is supposed to be, she seems not nearly as sick as the tiny premmie babies that occupy the humidicribs nearby. The paediatric cardiologist appears beside me, checking to see how my baby has managed the transition from the relative safety of the womb. He listens to her heart through the stethoscope and takes in her face, which is remarkably pink.

"If you didn't know, you wouldn't know," he says. "She might not need the Prostaglandin until tomorrow."

He's referring to the medication needed to keep the ductus arteriosus open. While useful in utero, this blood vessel is designed to close naturally soon after birth. For Jayne, though, ensuring it remains patent is the first step in saving her life, at least until the surgeon can operate on her walnut-sized heart in a few days' time.

After the cardiologist disappears into the cold night, I watch my daughter sleep, reluctant to leave her and return to my room. We cannot be sure how the next weeks and months will unfold, but I have this moment with her. I lean in, inhale her newborn scent and wrap my hand around soft, tiny fingers.

My Tent

NATALIE CHER LEITÃO

My tent is a defiant toddler
on the white coastal sands.
She balls her fists and wildly kicks,
fighting to maintain her composure as strong breezes unsettle her.
I pack her up and move on.

Camping in Ningaloo I am both citizen and tourist
*   as I traverse this country,*
mesmerised by the vast coastline; hues of turquoise and teal
*   edged by pure white.*
Bathing simultaneously in sunshine and salt water I drift
*   alongside angelfish and turtles.*
This is the Ningaloo life: woken by morning kiss of the dawning sun,
*   comforted by blanket of stars at night.*

My tent is an old woman, gentle and serene
on the red compacted earth.
The breeze causes her to lift and exhale,
sighing softly while she keeps me safe within her embrace.
I pack her up and move on.

Camping in Karijini I am both citizen and tourist
*   as I traverse this country,*
transfixed by outstretched red plains
*   that are scorched by the sun,*
refreshed by blue-green waterfalls that gush and pool
*   across ancient rocks.*
This is the Karijini life: woken by morning kiss of the dawning sun,
*   comforted by blanket of stars at night.*

A Mother's Fairytale

ELLA KURZ

one   had eaten the sun
    saw dreams in the sky
    smelt of creamed honey

the other   carried the moon
      made the air wobble
      befriended the snails

their existence
    took more than she was
    took what she was

she bore her trials –
dragon tears
witches' kisses
dark slumber

          as they all do
with silence on her lips

until she was   free
   heard herself
         laughing
music returned lightness was hers

and she remembered
to press her cheek against their soft
warm faces   at dawn and at dusk

A Game of Anything

ANDREW LANSDOWN

I am watching two little girls
like ducklings tottering

in line behind their mother—
only, they are making a game

of the going, taking care
with wing-flappings for balance

to keep in the lanky shadow
she is casting on the asphalt

as she trundles her trolly
in the late afternoon sunlight

through the shopping-centre carpark.

Essence

ALCHENNY AGYPUTRI

A faint smell of latex gloves mixes in with the scent of freshly waxed, white floors. The electronic bell chimes whenever the door opens and closes. An instrumental piece plays in the background, with the same seven notes in rotation. Suburban gossip fills the air.

Welcome to Topland Scoop 'n' Weigh.

Take any, take all. If not 100% satisfied, give us a call.

We provide you with ... your pride and joy!

Topland's marketing line has lived in my head rent-free ever since I started working for them five years ago. Now I'm in my 30s, acting as the store manager in our High Okane branch. Every time a customer comes in and asks, "Can I speak to the manager?" my immediate instinct is to hide my work badge, wanting to escape the Complaints Saga.

Oh well, I can't blame them for having high expectations of our store. After all, what makes Topland Scoop 'n' Weigh so different from other scoop and weigh shops is that we don't just sell foods such as organic pine nuts sourced from Brazil or specially milled non-GMO buckwheat flour. No, we sell 'Essence' available as pills and tablets. No prescriptions are needed. Just scoop, weigh, and be on your merry way.

"Excuse me. Could I speak to your manager, please?"

Uh oh, here we go.

"Good evening, Ma'am. Can I help you?" I say, grinning from ear to ear.

"Well, you better. My son bought some of your Confidence Essence last night for a job interview. Not only did he fail it, but now he's acting up towards me and my husband!"

"How so?"

"He kept treating us like some servants, being obnoxious and rude. I don't know what happened to my sweet boy! I demand a refund!"

"How many Essence pills did he take?"

"I ... He took five pills. How is that relevant? I want my refund!"

I shake my head. "Sounds like an overdose of Confidence, Ma'am. We specifically wrote the recommended dosage on the label."

The customer frowns. "Are you trying to shift the blame onto us?"

"Not at all, Ma'am. However, I do think this is an easy fix." I smile. I pack a couple of pills in a Ziploc bag and hand it to her. "Get your son to take one pill of our Humility Essence this evening and one tomorrow morning, with plenty of water. He should return to normal by then. It's on the house."

She scoffs. "Fine, but if that doesn't happen, you'll see me again soon." She walks away, leaving a threatening tone in the air.

Essence. Forty years after The Pandemic, scientists moved on from attempts in prolonging life to attempts to ultimately improve people's disposition and morality. They invented Essence. Feel a little bit down? Take 2 mg of our Joy Essence and feel like yourself again! Have intrusive thoughts about yourselves and others? Take 5 mg of our Wisdom Essence and avoid making decisions you'll regret! The chemicals in each type of Essence send signals to your brain—it amplifies or tones down your traits according to various needs. Thanks to Essence, the national crime rates have gone down by 97.8%.

Topland Corporation is the biggest sponsor for the research of Essence. In exchange for ongoing research funds, Topland has the sole commercial rights to Essence. After witnessing the positive effects of our products on customers' lives, I can truly vouch that Essence is humanity's greatest invention.

My thoughts are interrupted as I notice a young man looking around the store nervously. I approach him. "Good evening, Sir. Can I help you with anything?"

He glances at me—his hands are trembling. He pulls his mask up as he bolts towards the door, but he bumps into the security barrier near it. Piles of Ziploc bags spill out of his hoodie. I check the label. Restraint Essence.

"Please! I don't have any money, but I need them!" the man yells.

"Sir, calm down—"

"Don't call the police on me! Let me explain."

"Sir, it's alright. Get up. Let's talk this out at the back."

The shoplifter explains to me that ever since he was young, he had a habit of stealing. It grew worse as he grew in age. What started as stealing his friend's lunch money turned into more serious things: pick-pocketing, carjacking, then embezzling funds at work. As soon as he started taking Restraint Essence, his urges faded away. Unfortunately, he was fired from work after the embezzlement came to light. With no money and Essence left, his old habits resurfaced immediately.

"Please. I promise I won't do this anymore. I *just* need this Essence," the man says.

I ponder. I hand him two doses of Restraint Essence and a piece of paper. "I can only give you this much. This is a voucher that you can use for next time, *but* if you try to steal from us again, you'll regret it."

The man lights up. "Thank you!" He shakes my hand and then bows profusely before leaving.

I place a hand on my head. Restraint Essence is supposed to be the strongest Essence, even with just one dose. Prisoners are given two doses each month during rehabilitation, with 90% of them showing no sign of criminal urges afterwards. Even *murderers* can eventually resettle into society, only needing to take one every year as maintenance. It's the reason why our crime rate has gone down so much. How can this man need *more* if his urge is only to steal?

"Maybe his body's more resistant towards the chemicals in Essence," I mutter, trying to explain it to myself. I write a detailed report of the incident, as well as my concerns and suggestions. I'm sure our products need only a *little* bit of adjustment and they will become even more effective. I send my report to the director, Mrs Choi. Shortly after, I receive a phone call.

"Bennett, you're coming with me to Fleur this Saturday."

"For what occasion, Mrs Choi?"

"We've been thinking of including you in the larger scheme of things. You and I are meeting Topland's President and the Chief Researcher of Essence."

She hangs up. I stare at the wall, trying to process our brief conversation. Are they *that* moved by my report?

For the next few days, I find myself immersed in administrative duties—albeit my mind is still preoccupied with the shoplifting incident. Before heading to Fleur with Mrs Choi, I need to make sure that the store will be up and running in tiptop shape during my absence. Time flies quickly even with boring paperwork when you know something thrilling is coming once you're done.

Saturday arrives. With it, Mrs Choi and I arrive at Essence Research Centre in Fleur. Trying to contain my excitement, I bite my lip as I grip my jacket sleeves tightly.

The research centre is different from what I've imagined. It's splashed with muggy brown and grey colours. The wooden double doors don't mesh well with the unpolished, prickly concrete walls and floors. Rather than a research centre, the place looks more like an odd combination of an office and a military base. You can't see or even hear what people in the other rooms are up to. There are multiple elevators, with each one corresponding to a specific floor. Mrs Choi and I reach the seventh floor, our meeting place with the President and Chief Researcher.

"Ah, Mrs Choi. Welcome."

A man in his 50s is standing in the middle of the hallway. The shiny bald spot on his head makes the thin strands of grey hair surrounding it barely noticeable. He's wearing a burgundy three-piece suit. Beside him is a woman in a lab coat, her brunette hair neatly tucked in a bun. We walk closer to them.

"Good afternoon, President Adams, Mrs Lorez," Mrs Choi says and gestures to me. "This is Bennett, the one I mentioned to you before."

"Ah, Bennett, yes," President Adams scans me up and down before smiling. "Welcome."

Mrs Lorez chimes in. "Please, come into the conference room."

President Adams sits in the furthest chair in the room. He leans back. "So, Bennett, tell me, how have you found working for us?"

His sudden question flusters me. "Well, Sir, I feel honoured to have been with Topland for five years. I know all the ins and outs of the stores. I know the details of every single Essence … " I ramble on, telling him how much I admire the company, " … It's especially been a privilege to see how much Essence has helped the customers who come to our store."

He smiles. "Hm, I admire your passion. For Essence and Topland."

"Thank you, Sir. However, a recent incident has been on my mind." I explain to him the shoplifting incident. I propose that certain Essence products can be further developed by tweaking them to match different people's genetic makeup. "I've been thinking of different ways to improve Essence and make them more well-received, Sir."

Silence fills the room.

"Mrs Choi, you chose the right person. I'm sure he can be part of the next step," President Adams says. He turns to me, "Why don't the both of you rest up at the hotel now? Come back tomorrow and we'll chat about the next step."

Mrs Choi and I leave the centre. At the hotel, I shuffle through all the TV channels, thinking about what exactly the "next step" may be. Will I become an owner of multiple branches? Perhaps the head of the marketing department? Or will I get to be a part of the research?

Excitement, nervousness, and disorientation muddle my brain resulting in a sleepless night.

The next day, we return. President Adams and Mrs Lorez escort us to a different section of the centre. We enter a fairly empty room. On one side of the wall, there's a wide rectangular window with red curtains draping over them. Cold air seeps through the walls, making me shiver slightly. A few office chairs are set up in the middle of the room. Is this an interview room?

"Mr Bennett, we'll discuss the next step for you here," Mrs Lorez says as she opens the curtain, revealing a mirror instead of a window. She presses a button and it flips, making the other side of the room visible. Ah, it's one of those one-way mirrors. Are they going to make me get in that room and do some sort of interrogation-style interview? A bit unconventional.

I step closer to the one-way mirror. I clam up as I look through properly, the cold air once again seeping through the walls. The other side is not empty. It's not set up for an interview.

Men and women dressed in orange jumpsuits are laid down on steel beds.

"What ... is this?" I ask.

"Prisoners," President Adams say. "Dead prisoners, to be exact."

"I don't understand."

"This is how we handle *imperfections*," he replies.

"I'm afraid I still don't understand, Sir."

President Adams positions himself next to me. "Look, you said you wanted to make Essence more *well-received*. We're showing you the inner workings of Topland right now. We get rid of imperfections."

"Sir, if by imperfections you mean these people, then that's too extreme. Even if rehabilitation with Essence doesn't work on them, we can make adjustments to match with their—"

President Adams smirks. "Their genetic makeup?"

"Mr Bennett," Mrs Lorez pauses, "Have you ever *tried* Essence?"

"Why yes, of course. I don't take them regularly, but I've taken Restful Essence a few times before and they worked perfectly."

"Have you received any complaints about our products not functioning?" Mrs Lorez asks.

"Well, yes, but I'd explain to them how Essence works in the body and how to take them properly. I'd make adjustments based on that. They always come back saying it works perfectly for them, too."

I look around to see everyone's blank expression. I continue, "Sir, as I was saying, with my knowledge of Essence, we can find a better solution than ... getting rid of people with resistance towards the chemicals in Essence—"

President Adams roars in laughter. "Bennett, do you need me to spell it out for you?" he pauses, "Essence isn't *real*. Have you never heard of the placebo effect?"

I stay silent.

He continues, "Get your head out of the clouds! This isn't some trashy sci-fi novel. Did you *really* think we can change people from the inside out with some pills?"

The room starts to feel blurry. The insides of my stomach are turning.

"The barcode in Essence packaging helped us track our society's ... *bad apples*. We monitor them, bribe them, force them to change their outward behaviour." President Adams grabs a marker from his pocket, drawing a line on the mirror. "If they fail to keep up their game, well ..." he crosses out the dead prisoners' faces on the mirror.

"But ... how?" I ask. Not out of curiosity nor contempt, but pure confusion.

"Easy. Showcase the ones that managed to keep a clean record and get them to write testimonials. Once people are convinced that Essence works for the bigger stuff, they'll swallow up the little things." He chuckles. "Confidence for a job interview, relaxation for the night, you name it."

This doesn't make any sense. Can the placebo effect go this far? What about the police? How come I *never* hear of *any* suspicion?

The President stares at me. "You seem like your brain's overheating. Want some Restful Essence?" he asks in a mocking tone.

"It's ... it's just not possible."

"Oh, but it is. You underestimate people's minds—they believe what they *want* to believe. Combine that with my power and money, it's an easy road from there."

I clench my fists. "You're a sick bastard."

"*I'm* sick? I'm just helping the world clean up garbage." He gestures towards the dead prisoners. "Keeping up peace and morale, all while earning even more money. Have you forgotten our marketing line? *We provide you with your pride and joy.* How is this sick? It's *genius*, and I'm inviting you in on it."

"Never," I say, gritting my teeth. "I'll expose you for this."

"Oh? Well, if you're so righteous, let me give you two choices: Will you be the face of Essence, keeping up good morale, giving people the freedom to live happily with the ease of comfort or will you expose everything, ruining people's lives by robbing them of their hope to live a peaceful life?"

No, that's not right. He's twisting logic. Right? I won't be robbing anyone of anything.

The relieved shoplifter comes to mind.

Hundreds of customers that thanked me come to mind.

My friends who feel at peace come to mind.

I ...

"Hm, you don't seem so sure anymore," the President says.

Unable to keep myself steady, I fall to the ground.

The President places a chair in front of me and sits down with his arms crossed. He leans forward, staring down at me.

"So ... What will it be, Bennett?"

Scripture Reading

HOR SHIDE GYATSO
(TRANS MIKE RANDALL)

དཔེ་ཆ་ཀློག་པ།

དཔེ་ཆ་ཀློག་པ་ནི་སྐྱོ་སྣང་ཟབ་པ་ཡིན།
དཔེ་ཆ་ཀློག་པ་ནི་འོད་སྣང་འཁྱུང་བ་ཡིན།

དཔེ་ཆ་ཀློག་པ་ནི་སེམས་ལ་མེ་ཏོག་འཇུགས་པ་ཡིན།
དཔེ་ཆ་ཀློག་པ་ནི་སྙིང་ལ་སྐྱང་རྩེ་འདེབས་པ་ཡིན།

དཔེ་ཆ་ཀློག་པ་ནི་ཡམ་རང་གིས་བཏོ་བ་ཡིན།
དཔེ་ཆ་ཀློག་པ་ནི་ཀློག་རང་གིས་གཅོད་པ་ཡིན།

To read scripture is to consume pleasure,
To read scripture is to drink brilliant light,

To read scripture is to plant a flower in your heart,
To read scripture is to sow honey in your mind,

To read scripture is to forge your own path,
To read scripture is to cut through your own snares.

To Logan, A Child with San Filippo Syndrome

ALEXANDRA JUSTINICO

He is forgetting how to speak,
he is forgetting how to walk,
he is forgetting how to hug,
he is forgetting how to eat.

The regression started when he was two,
we knew we would lose him since he was two.

He is losing his mind,
what a pain to see him lose himself,
he is losing his body,
what a pain to see him fade away.

> **He is just a child!**
> **HE IS JUST A CHILD THAT HAS ALREADY**
> **STARTED TO DIE!**
> **He is just a child!**
> **HE IS JUST A CHILD WITH NO FUTURE IN SIGHT!**

His body is not giving him a chance,
nature is not giving him a chance,
God is not giving him a chance.

His body is unable to let him live
unable to let him learn, unable to keep him here.
He will leave before me, before his dad,
before having a chance to build a life.

Like Alzheimer's in children they say
There is no hope they say!
There is no cure they say!
Why him? Why us?
Why not even a chance?
The hardships of a child with a terminal illness
the physical toll, the mental toll,
on him, on us, on the world.
NO CHILD SHOULD DIE THAT YOUNG!
Hopeless, unfairness, wrongness.
NO CHILD SHOULD BE WITHOUT HOPE!

Does he know he is dying?
He is thirteen he must know!
Does he know he is regressing?
His brain is 18 months old, he doesn't know.
Is there justice in the world?

We find joy with what we have,
look at his smile,
look at his eyes,
look at his bushy eyebrows,
look at his full lips
look at his innocence
look at his joy, look at his love.
Could we learn to be so pure?

I would trade my life for his,
but it's not how it works
IT IS NOT HOW IT WORKS!

We will make him as happy as we can,
we will be here to enjoy him.
we will enjoy him as much as we can,
we will be here to love him,
we will create dear memories to hold.

And when he is gone,
his memory will keep us fighting for a cure,
his memory will help us to survive
his memory will remind us to be sure,
that even with the unfairness in the world,
there is still beauty to be found,
there are still reasons to fight for.

You are a blessing condemned to leave us soon,
But a blessing is a blessing,
your smile is a blessing,
your existence is a blessing,
No matter how soon you go,
your transit in this world has purpose.
Could the world someday learn to be so pure?

The Homecoming

ANDREW LANSDOWN

1

Restraint

As the car pulls up
the pup goes prancing to the door
to greet my grandkids.
Though I stay put, I too feel like
yapping and rolling on the floor.

2

Anticipation

I hear the dog greet
my grandchildren in the drive.
Shortly, they'll enter
my study with jostle and shove
and paw at me for scraps of love.

Train to Newcastle

MAYA KRAYNEVA

There is something cosy about being on a train. Maybe, it's the lullaby song of wheels along the rails, or the cradle of carriages rocking subtly, or the opportunity to rest and progress at the same time.

The train to Newcastle was like the trains I had been on, Brussels to Antwerp being the most frequent. The main difference was the amount of people on the train. There was just one man in the carriage with plenty of empty seats around us, as if they were reserved for the ghosts of my past. Too many times I have heard, *You can run away from a place, but you can never run away from yourself.*

The seat facing me was empty too. After the long flight from Brussels to Sydney, with a stopover in Kuala Lumpur, the seat appeared very tempting. As if it was inviting me, presenting itself to me, introducing itself to me as a footrest. In my mind, I was justified, convinced to accept the seat's offer. So, I lifted my feet and gave the seat an opportunity to serve me. My feet thanked me.

We had left Sydney and were passing through a smaller town along the way. "Woy, Woy," came through the speaker. *What? Is this a place?* I wondered. Then I saw a sign, and yes, Woy Woy was a place. *Such an unusual name Woy Woy! Does it mean anything?*

The houses outside resembled my grandmother's home in Bosnia; freestanding, with a small garden around. They were unlike houses in Belgium which share a wall with each other.

The trees though were dissimilar to the ones in Europe. They were shorter, smaller, and appeared thorny. They were nothing like the trees at my grandmother's place in Bosnia—trees with long branches that scraped the ground and gently stroked my face when I happened to fall asleep underneath them.

Sleep, sleep, sleep. My body urged my mind to calm down and give it some rest, but I couldn't. I couldn't fall asleep on the plane, and I couldn't find a few moments of rest on this two-and-half hour long journey to Newcastle. How could I? I was thinking about my mum and my brother, and the last time I saw them. I had waved them goodbye not knowing when I would see them next. And now, that moment of seeing them was just in front of me.

Deep in my thoughts, I didn't hear the carriage door open behind me. The conductor appeared in front of me, pointing his index finger at my feet. I felt guilty even before he spoke.

"Sorry," I said and put my feet down.

"It's Ok," he said, "you can keep your feet up, just take off your shoes."

I dared not to think how my socks would smell after the long flight. "It's Ok," I said. "Here is my ticket."

The conductor glanced at my ticket and gave it back to me. "All good. Thank you." He moved over to the elderly man sitting a few seats away from me.

The man was wearing white socks underneath his woven sandals. *Socks and sandals, you never wear them together*, are the instructions I was given as a child. But this man seemed to have been given different instructions. His socks also matched his shirt and his beige shorts. And even more, his outfit matched his ginger hair and freckles.

"Thank you," the conductor said to him and continued walking through the train.

"Put your feet up," the elderly man said. "I can see your bags, and it looks like you have come from overseas."

"Yes, it's true. I flew in from Brussels this morning."

"On a holiday or working?" The man moved a seat closer. The smell of his cologne washed over me.

"Visiting my family," I answered. "Does your family live in Australia too?"

"My daughter lives in Melbourne. She is a lawyer. But my son, he lives in Washington. He works at the University. And I have five grand-children, four boys and one girl."

"You sound like my grandfather. I was my grandfather's only girl amongst six boys. He called me his princess." The sun lit my face as I contemplated the sweetest memories of my past, long before my parent's divorce and the war.

He smiled. "I am Garry, by the way."

"Maya; nice to meet you, Garry." Dry patched skin on this man's face spoke of Australian sun—the same sun that introduced itself by warmly shaking my hand through the window.

"Nice to meet you too, Maya," Garry said. "How long you will be staying here?"

"I don't know. I just know I need to see my mum and my brother. I haven't thought much about what will happen afterwards."

"When was the last time you saw them?" he asked.

"Almost four years ago, at Brussels Airport."

The man's eyebrows lifted. "Why didn't you come with them back then?"

"I stayed in Belgium to finish my studies." My gaze dropped as I remembered the lasting struggle in Belgium on my own. The hope of finishing my studies and seeing my mother and my brother again had been a continual source of light along the dark tunnel of grey skies, rainy days, and never-ending loneliness.

"Belgium? You do not sound Belgian. And you do not look Belgian." He took a tissue from his pocket and wiped sweat from his forehead.

"Yes, it is confusing, even for me. I have Belgian nationality and a Belgian passport, but I was born in another country—a country that doesn't exist anymore."

"Which country?" Garry asked, "I thought you were Russian."

"Why? Do I look Russian?"

"Polish?" the man continued querying.

"No."

"I know," the man raised his arm as he said, "You are Serbian! My neighbours sound just like you."

"Mmmm ..." I was scratching my head while seeking for the right answer. "Half-Serbian," was the best I could find. "My mum is Serbian but my dad, he is Muslim."

"Muslim? How Muslim? Being Muslim is not a nationality; it is a religion."

"Ahh, yes, you are right. I never saw this before." This man's words fell on me like a weighted blanket. There was something comforting about them, as if they had brought me closer to answers about nationality and religion. Even though, at the same time, they opened up a range of new mysteries to me.

"I don't understand the religious part either," I continued. "I was born in Yugoslavia while Tito was in power. I was told that religion is only for old people who never went to school and could not understand the world by science. My dad told me that uneducated people interpreted thunder as God being angry and yelling at people."

The man chuckled. "Was your dad an angry man?"

"Actually, he was," I answered and joined this man's laughter, although I didn't know why; there was nothing funny about the memories of my dad's anger. But this man's happiness was contagious, and I was too tired to think too hard and be too serious about all that happened before.

"Tell me again," the man said. "Why were you guys fighting over there? News was always blurry."

"I don't know. Even to this day, I don't understand," I said. "I am half-Serbian and half-Muslim ... sorry, half-Bosniak. It would be like one part of me killing the other part."

My own words arrested my attention. *Could this be a reason for the constant fight between my feelings and my thoughts*, I wondered. *The great disconnect that has existed in me for most of my life?*

I felt like depression and sadness stood in my way. As a way of coping, I had decided to deny my feelings a voice. They were silenced like a woman in a marriage, being a part of the whole, yet having her voice denied. And soon, my body had started protesting too. A divide between my mind, emotions, and body established itself within me, and it grew stronger with every year that passed by. The division within was also a constant source of tension waiting to burst and break me in pieces anytime.

But there was nothing tense about this man. With a gentle smile on his face, he was quite content. He appeared as an ordinary man, yet his words were profound and caused me to rethink my ways.

Noticing I had been quiet for a while, Garry said, "Sorry, I didn't mean to upset you in any way."

"No, you didn't. I am just thinking." Garry's words were freeing me, as if calling me out of a self-made cocoon. A cocoon I knew too well. It wasn't a healthy place to inhabit, but it was familiar. The longer I spent on my own, the thicker the walls of this cocoon would become—as if it was trying to kill me, the caterpillar inside, prematurely.

"Were Croatians also involved in the war?" Garry continued.

"Yes. Serbians, Bosniaks, and Croatians were all fighting against each other."

"Just because they were not of the same *nation* as the others?" the man asked as if he struggled to believe me.

"Or not of the same *religion* as the others," I added. "Serbians are Orthodox, Bosniaks are Muslim, and Croatians are Catholics." I was trying to make connections and understand things as I spoke.

"Can a Croatian person choose Orthodox or Muslim religion?" Garry asked.

"I don't know," I answered. "I have never heard of anything like that."

"And you, what is your religion?"

"None!" A flash of irritation furrowed my brows. "I have seen some of these religious people cross themselves and offer prayers to God, and then go and kill others just because they are of a different religion, or nationality, as them. I don't desire their religion."

"I see," Garry nodded. "Do you believe God exists?"

"I believe in something. I would go to a church in Belgium on Sundays and light up a candle. I would pray to God to help me with exams and bring me to Australia to see my mother and my brother."

Garry beamed. "He surely heard your prayers."

"Yes, He did," I said and looked outside.

Purple branches of passing trees gave rest to my eyes. And my soul. *Rest, peace, and sleep. That is what I need.*

"What are those beautiful trees?" I asked. "I've never seen them before."

"Jacarandas," he said. "They light up our streets every spring."

It was September and spring in Australia. The birth of a new season, a new beginning, and possibly a new life for me.

Song of the Seasons

NAMLOYAK DHUNGSER

The wind that is flying anywhere.
A poem like the singing of the wind.
The wind must play with music.
A piece of music in an old poem.

An old poem that opens a door.
The door opens up and embraces the spring.
Spring sends a bird: a message to the forest.
A tree starts to smile with unfurling green.

The green writes down the colour of the earth.
The earth wears the clothing of spring.
A hand raised and beckoning to summer.
Summer, revelling in the arms of the sun.

The sun peers back from the horizon.
The horizon lifts up yellow autumn.
Who knows whether yellow is a legend or a poem?
This poem is a leaf proposing love to the busy wind.

Bangus at Karagatan / Milkfish and Ocean

ALISON DENCH

For my Tagalog language teacher

Kamakailan lamang
'di namamalayan

ay ngumingiti ako
sa wikang Pilipino

isang ngisi:

kulubot na manlalakbay,
hubog at siksik
may kulay

'tulad ng mga
basang
kaliskis
ng bangus

at
malawak sa kagandahan
bilang isang karagatan

palagi
kahit na ano
nginginitian ninyo ako.

Lately
unconsciously

I'm smiling
in Filipino (language)

a broad smile:

corrugated traveller,
curved and crammed
with colour

like the
water-soaked
scales
of milkfish.

Expansive in beauty
as an ocean
always
no matter what
you smile (back) at me.

Ants

STEPHANIE FELIX

For Jake

Warm afternoon winds caress
ants climbing limestone steps.
In a flame tree's whispering foliage
red-winged fairy-wrens gossip.
I tickle the buffalo turf.

My love lies beside me lifting,
with a crisp fallen leaf, an errant worker
from the dark chocolate field
of his hand's hairs to its persistent colony,
encapsulating *To Kill a Mockingbird.*

Cars, like old arguments, pass.
Advancing ants carry the heavy gold
of sticky honeydew bounties
to their impatient queen. Here, still,
for now, our peaceful silence.

Hours later, a stale breeze
carries a MAGA bike rider
past freshly built estates
into our safe distance;
marking off-white pavement with black tar.

By now, the sun moves
amongst canary yellow
African daisies, drops
behind grey stones;
gone, like birdsong,

to a new neighbourhood. Remembering
this, I close my eyes, leaving
waking street lights behind to dream
of our ants in cool descending tunnels
on our homeward drive.

What Spears Are Good For

BEN LEE

Oscar

Sunrise bathes the land in oranges and pinks, and touches the tufts of Oscar's black hair which stick out like a pair of thick horns. The scenery looks like those pictures of Mars, not like the earth at all. He sits, legs shoved between metal spires, feet dangling over the cliff, spear in hand. Mum's at the window, watching, even though he's told her not to. No-one needs to worry about him – the wrought-iron fence keeps him from the worn edge, maybe the worn edge from him. Below him the forest lies in shadow, a great yawning mouth. Sometimes he hears the sound of skittering, or gulping, slithery-wet sounds. He wonders what the beast really looks like, where it came from, whether it smells the tips of his toes. He's not afraid. But he can't go to the forest until he's a man, that's what Mum says, so maybe in a few years, when he's twelve? Then he can hunt like Dad did.

He doesn't look at the sun anymore. The sting of Mum's smack is still fresh on his behind. He gets lots of smacks. Mum says that smacks are good if they keep you from going blind, and some fences are good if they keep you from the death below. But Oscar never likes smacks and he doesn't like fences he can't climb over. He rasps the soles of his feet against his legs, shaking off the dirt. He's been here two days already, and all he's seen are sunrises behind bars.

A shout in the distance. Oscar gets up and runs to the house for breakfast. He goes past a fire with a giant pot on it and hops over the broken middle step to the door. The flyscreen door batters against the weatherboards, teal paint flaking off. He sits down and starts pouring milk into his cereal before getting a slap on the back of his hand.

"Wash first," says Mum, her spoon raised. Her voice cuts the air but her wide eyes are almost comical and take any sting out of the smack. Oscar goes off and comes back, wiping his hands on his pants, and spoons the wheat flakes into his mouth. Another spoon to his hand.

"What are we forgetting?"

"In food, in danger, in love, and in pain," said Oscar, rolling his eyes, "Thank the Lord in Jesus's name."

"You're staying upstairs for the rest of the day," she says. She points at his face. "Not a *word*." Her eyes unfocus, though only for a moment. "It's not punishment. We have to keep safe for the day. Dark's coming, after all." Her voice is different, her eyes sharp. He nods. She takes his bowl and spoon and heads out the back door. Oscar takes his spear and watches Mum from the downstairs back window. With a ladle and a smaller pot, she draws hot water from the pot outside, then returns, proceeds to pour it into the sink to wash the dishes. Satisfied, Oscar climbs upstairs, slapping at the triangular holes in the wall.

Why does the dark come so fast? Oscar stares out the window down at the cliff edge now in shade, as is the fence and the yawning forest beyond. Mum is right; already the shadows have shifted so fast. There's something not right about the shadows or the way time has gone so fast here in the two days since they arrived. They left behind nearly everything, took only some clothes, some knives, pots and pans, a couple of suitcases. And the spear. Mum said he wasn't to take it. She didn't win that one. How could he leave Dad behind? He got lots of smacks for that, but she didn't take it from him.

There. A shift in the woods like a drifting blanket among the trees, and a flash of red. Oscar feels the shaft of the spear in his hand, the grain smooth where his father's hand once held it. He pushes the rough butt of the spear against the top of his foot, thinking. He can't go outside, that's what Mum said, and yet ... that was an eye he saw out there, challenging him. He sneaks downstairs, looks down the corridor to the back of the house. From the back comes the scent of onions, the heady warmth of a stew coming along – but at the front of the house, a knitting needle drops onto the floor. Oscar looks both ways, and in that moment turns to the back door.

Jo

"Oscar! Dinner in 10!"

She tosses the needles on the armchair, gives up on the attempt. It's the most pointless thing in the world, to knit a shawl in your last days. Jo walks out the back to stir the pot outside. It's a race against the sun – the steam envelops her view of the impending dusk. She tastes her work, nearly burning her tongue, but the stew is nearly ready. They didn't have much time to leave; this was the only place she could think of, from memory no less. The darkness swallows everything in sight, and she wonders why she even tries – there are things you simply cannot escape from. But when the reports came on the TV she thought of only one thing, and that was the wild-haired boy asleep on her lap, to spend her last days with him. A few more days, or even one. If only there were better places than this.

There are three darknesses, or maybe they're all one. There's the creature, moving from East to West, preferring the shadows. The rot it leaves behind has a life of its own, desolation in its wake, consuming, sapping life from everything. And all the while the days are shortening – each slow, like a glacier, but fast enough to scare anyone to move.

This is where Jo grew up, the westernmost place she knows. She had left it as soon as she could when she was old enough. There's the middle step where her father beat her till it cracked. There are notches throughout the walls inside, places he took to with a hatchet. He wasn't well, and sometimes he forgot to take his meds. There were good days when nothing happened, and bad days when everything happened.

The sun is low now. She knows she shouldn't stare, but lately the sun seems to have lost something of itself. It almost feels safe to look at it directly, perhaps a by-product of the darkness. She takes the pot by the handles and shifts it to one side, onto a set of breezer blocks. That's when she notices the upstairs window, the light is not on. That kid. Always leave the light on, that's what she's told Oscar, and used the spoon to remind him. She goes in and upstairs to remind him again.

He's not there.

Jo bursts out the back, calling for Oscar, but the sky is smoky, pressing in. She manages to take the pot inside, then shuts every window, turns every light on. She takes her trusty meat cleaver and a butterfly lantern. She turns to the left before the cliff edge, down a half-hidden path, picking her way down, down, down towards the forest. She doesn't want to go this way again, but she has to. Oscar is her son, and that's all there is to say.

Oscar

He should never have come here. Oscar sees the first real view of the sky in some time. Already the clouds are tainted with oily brown and even the clearing is dark, trees rising high. In the centre of the clearing is a burned-up frame, a skeleton of a cabin of some kind. Spear still in hand, Oscar uses the sharp flint blade to shave off some bits of wood from a branch. You need kindling to start a fire, that much he knows from his time in the cub scouts, and something to light it. He doesn't know how he's going to do that, but he'll find a way. Maybe. The shavings form a small pile in the centre of a bunch of sticks.

Once Oscar threw the spear at Dad. It was never going to hit, but he wasn't paying attention to what his dad was saying and then the spear flew out of his hand and landed in the dirt somewhere in Dad's direction. As punishment, he had to hold the spear, arms out straight until he couldn't do it anymore. Then Dad sat him down and wiped his arms with a wet cloth.

"Son, do you know what spears are good for?" Dad said.

"For throwing. And killing a pig. For dinner."

"Yes. But they are only good when we use them right. What you did today, was it the right thing to do?"

"No, Dad."

"And why was that?"

"Because I tried to kill you." Oscar felt the tears in his eyes.

"When you misused the spear, in that moment it was good for nothing." Oscar winced as Dad wiped away at a cut. "What will you do different next time? How will you make the spear do good?"

"I—I'm going to listen to you."

"That's right,' said Dad. "See here?" he pointed to the left part of his chest. "If this is right, then the spear will be right." He handed the spear to Oscar. "Take care of it till I get back from duty, okay? We have to fight something over on the east coast."

* * *

A sound penetrates the place, again. Oscar freezes. That skittering sound, and the wet, slithery one, same as a moment ago, and when he was back at the house. Why didn't he listen to Mum? A gust of wind throws dust in his eyes, and whips the shavings into the air. He opens one eye and sees, there in the shadows of the trees, that same shifting mass of darkness. Then a red shape opens and stares at him. It is an eye after all, and below that an impossibly large mouth, and fangs. Oscar can barely hold onto his spear. The eye turns. Something comes out of the trees towards him, and at once Oscar knows this is how he is going to die. He crouches, the spear in front, but he can't see anything—the tears are in the way.

Oscar still can't see through all the tears. The wind is growing stronger. He stands at the ready, the head of the spear in front. He can hear the beat of his heart, thumping loudly. He knows he doesn't have a good heart because he gets smacks all the time. This is it, he's going to die. Suddenly the air stops. Oscar throws up his arms, spear in full swing, and cries out the only name he knows when he's in danger, then falls to the ground. The air rushes in again. There's a loud, snapping sound, then a loud shriek, then all goes dark.

Jo

Oscar. She hears the screaming and the snap. Jo runs into the clearing, her cleaver at the ready – but there's no need. She holds the lantern over the place and can't believe what she sees. A long giant shape is coiled around a burned-out structure, some cabin from long ago, maybe belonging to a woodsman. The head of that shape is impaled with that spear, the shaft broken. And there on the ground is Oscar. She takes him and checks all over, but there aren't any scratches or cuts. He opens his eyes.

"Why don't you listen to me?" says Jo. "Why can't you stay inside?"

"I'm sorry, Mum." He looks over to the spear, its broken shaft. "Oh no, it's gone. I've ruined Dad."

"Oh, I don't know," says Jo, taking the spear head and looking it over. "The head's still good, just needs a new shaft. I'll show you how to make one. Now, come on."

They leave the clearing, Jo carrying her son up the path along the cliff face, lantern in one hand, spear and cleaver in the other. The lamp stutters; she can barely make out the path ahead. Jo wonders if this is the last light she'll ever see, and the moment is as good as any.

"In food, in danger, love, or pain—"

She doesn't know if they'll reach the house or the stew, but as light drains out of the day she feels the warmth of him in her arms, and that is enough.

CONTRIBUTORS

During her time at Curtin University, **Alchenny Agyputri** developed her interest and skills in creative writing. She explored different types of writing: poetry, short stories, travel writing articles, and many more. Alchenny has a particular interest in writing dystopian and horror-themed stories, as well as experimental poetry. Her main aim in writing is not only to entertain, but to spark discussions about societal issues—taking readers along on a journey of perspectives through the lens of diverse characters.

Jackson Black lives in Perth, Western Australia. He is currently completing his History Honours at the University of Western Australia and holds a Bachelor of Arts majoring in History and Creative Writing from Sheridan Institute. He loves to write, except when he is staring at old documents, making 'one last trip' to a library or museum, playing tabletop wargames, or trying to improve his horsemanship.

Jillian Bretto is an Italo-Australian in her early twenties, who writes from Perth, Western Australia. She values her faith, family, and friends. She grew up on a steady diet of mystery novels and historical books from the public domain which shaped her love for period dramas and detective shows. Her goal is to learn Korean so she can watch Korean dramas without subtitles. Even though she has never seen Star Wars (which horrifies her friends) her dream is to one day own a Jedi stick (otherwise known as a lightsaber). She is a recent graduate of Sheridan Institute.

Alison Dench was born in England and moved to Australia as a child. She has always loved the sound of words. Her love of language has grown over the past 30 years while living and teaching in Australia, the Philippines, and Outer Mongolia. She currently lectures at Sheridan Institute of Higher Education, in Perth, giving academic writing support to all students.

Jake Dennis (www.poetofjazz.com) **Poetry:** *Art Monthly Australia, Cordite, Page Seventeen, Poetry NZ, Quadrant, Voiceworks, Westerly, Wet Ink*, etc. **Awards:** Eastwood/Hills Literary, Dorothea Mackellar, Mandurah Literary Prize, Now & Then: Literature Prize, Right Now: Human Rights, Roland Leach Poetry Prize, KSP Young Writer-in-Residence, The West Australian Young Writers Contest. **Guest Poet:** Cottonmouth, Voicebox, KSP Festival of the Asian-Australian Voice, Perth Poetry Club, WA Poetry Festival. **Screen/Stage:** *Beautiful Girls: The Bruno Mars Show* (Fringe World), *The Couch* (Foxtel), Madonna's *Rebel Heart* DVD, *The Glass Menagerie* (GRADS), *Like Blown Smoke* (DownStairs at The Maj), and *The Wrinkle Ranch* (Short + Sweet).

Namloyak Dhungser is a polyglot writer and a Tibetologist. Since 1999, he has authored 10 books in Tibetan and Chinese. He is currently a Bachelor of Arts student at Curtin University, majoring in Chinese and Creative Writing. His achievements in writing have been gained not by wishful thinking, but through hard work.

Born in Port Elizabeth, South Africa, **Stephanie Felix** worked at Felix Jewellers then graduated with a Certificate IV in Beauty Therapy (Queensland) before earning a Diploma of Beauty Therapy (Perth). After volunteering at St John of God hospice and training with Flex Health, Stephanie worked as a heath-care nurse assistant at Perth Children's Hospital and at St John of God (Murdoch and Midland). Stephanie was awarded Country Girl Management's "Biggest Inspirational

Girl" Runway Prize. She enjoys acting, baking, ballet, creative writing (memoir, poetry, prose), film, TV, gardening, op-shopping, painting, sewing, and singing.

Hor Shide Gyatso was born in the Malo area, Amdo, Tibet. While living in Tibet, he studied Tibetan grammar and composition, ancient Indian poetry, astrology, and geomancy. Outside of Tibet he has studied Tibetan logic, Paramita teachings, Madhyamaka, Abhidharma, and monastic ordinances, as well as Sanskrit and other subjects. While in India he taught grammar (at primary and high school level) as well as Tibetan composition. His poems, including "Small Satchel", "Narrow Path in Central Tibet", and "Hall of Belief", have been published in a range of journals. He is currently studying English in Australia.

Alexandra Justinico was born in Colombia and has lived in Australia for over seven years. She holds a Bachelor's degree in Architecture and is working on completing her Arts degree with a major in Creative Writing. She loves learning, feeling to the extreme, and helping others feel and connect. In addition, she is intrigued by the paradox that is the beauty and cruelty of life and reality.

Lakshmi R. Kanchi (aka SoulReserve) is a wistful poet. Her poetry explores love and its tumultuousness; fantasy and zest in nature; and allegories that provoke thought and evoke tender feelings. Read her published works in *Across Vast Horizons, Poetry d'Amour* (2019 & 2020), *Letters To Our Home, Recoil 12, Blue Bottle Journal, Burrow Journal, Brushstrokes II Anthology*, and *Creatrix*.

Maya Krayneva was born in Bosnia and Herzegovina (ex-Yugoslavia). When the civil war broke out in 1992, she moved to Belgium where she successfully completed high school and received a national scholarship to undertake university studies. Upon successful completion of the studies, she moved to Australia in 1999. She lived in Newcastle (NSW) for a few years before moving to Perth to undertake a doctoral degree at Curtin University. She stayed at Curtin for an additional five years as a Post-doctoral Research Fellow. Currently, Maya is working for Sheridan Institute of Higher Education where she also audits courses in Creative Writing. Maya is married to Nikita. They enjoy travel, outdoors, and exploring Bible mysteries together. They live in Perth with a few feathered friends.

Ella Kurz is a health researcher from Ngunnawal Country. In her doctoral studies she coined the term 'parturescence' to describe the possibilities childbearing offers for transformation. She co-edited the anthology *What We Carry: Poetry on Childbearing*, authored *My Mother is a Midwife* and received a special mention in The Bruce Dawes National Poetry Prize 2021.

Andrew Lansdown is a widely published and award-winning Australian writer whose works include three novels, two short story collections, one essay collection, two children's poetry collections, two photography-and-poetry collections and fifteen poetry collections. His most recent books are: *Kyoto Momiji Tanka: Poems and Photographs of Japan in Autumn* (Rhiza Press, 2019); and *Abundance: New and Selected Poems* (Wipf & Stock/ Cascade Books, 2020). *Abundance* was shortlisted for the 2021 Australian Christian Book of the Year Award. His website is: www.andrewlansdown.com

Ben Lee writes short stories and creative non-fiction. He was born in Australia, has lived in Hong Kong, and has family in both places. He has completed a Masters in Creative Writing at the University of Technology, Sydney. Ben loves playing the flute by ear and playing racquet sports. He has an awkward relationship with lawns.

Natalie Cher Leitão has always loved playing with words and has recently rediscovered the enjoyment of writing creatively. Inspiration struck unexpectedly in 2020 and 2021 while exploring the Pilbara and Kimberley on camping trips with her husband Rico. Natalie's day job involves writing that is formal and factual; for over two decades, re-search, reports, and record-keeping have been the product of two-finger typing on the keyboard. Now her fingers are taking baby steps as they learn to dance to a new rhythm.

Elizabeth Lewis is a published poet living in Perth, Western Australia. She has a degree in Writing and English, with Honours in Poetry, from Edith Cowan University. Elizabeth has worked in the book industry for over 20 years and chairs the board of the KSP Writers' Centre in the Perth Hills. Elizabeth loves wearing summer dresses and cooking Burmese curries from her Grandma's recipes.

Miriam Wei Wei Lo writes because life is too short and strange to let it pass without comment. Her work has been published in numerous journals and anthologies, including *Inscribe, The Anthology of Australian Prose Poetry* and *What We Carry: Poetry on Childbearing*. A second edition of her prize-winning first book, *Against Certain Capture*, was recently released by Apothecary Archive. She is of mixed Chinese-Malaysian and Anglo-Australian descent and lives, with her extended family, on Noongar country in Walyalup/Fremantle. She loves meditating on scripture as she runs along the beach. Find her on Insta @miriamweiweilo

Samuel Mitchell is a bank clerk. He has lived in the Nepean Valley since he was five. He is married to Yung Yung. They have three children. He is a follower of Jesus Christ. He enjoys reading, writing, food, hanging out, listening to music, drinking whisky, second-hand bookstores, deli-catessens, and being dispassionate.

Mike Randall lectures in Linguistics at Sheridan Institute of Higher Education. He has lived in six countries and taught in four of them. From phonology to poetry, Mike is interested in anything about language (and more importantly, the people who speak those languages).

T. C. Shelley has been writing short stories and poems for years. She started writing middle grade novels to entertain her daughter, who encouraged her to share her work with others. *The Boy Who Hatched Monsters* is the third book of her middle grade fantasy series and was released by Bloomsbury this year. She is a seasoned high school teacher and also lectures in Creative Writing at Sheridan Institute. She lives in Perth with her family and her two dogs.

Melinda Tognini's creative work has been published in magazines and anthologies in Australia and the US. Her first book, *Many Hearts, One Voice: the story of the War Widows' Guild in Western Australia,* was published by Fremantle Press in 2015. She teaches life writing and family history at the Sheridan Institute of Higher Education. She is currently a PhD candidate at Curtin University with the support of an Australian Government Research Training Program Scholarship.

Acknowledgements

Andrew Lansdown's "A Game of Anything" was first published in *Quadrant* (July-August 2021).

Andrew Lansdown's "The Homecoming" was first published in *This Gift, This Poem*, ed. Jean Kent, et al, Puncher & Wattmann, 2021.

www.ingramcontent.com/pod-product-compliance
Lightning Source LLC
Chambersburg PA
CBHW031956130726
47904CB00013B/2321